Go to Sleep, Gecko!

a Balinese folktale retold by
Margaret Read MacDonald
illustrated by **Geraldo Valério**

August House LittleFolk
LITTLE ROCK

One night Elephant was awakened.
He heard a loud noise right under his window.

"GECK-o! GECK-o! GECK-o!"

"Gecko, what are you doing here?
It is the middle of the night.
Go home and go to bed."

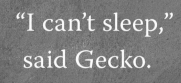

"I can't sleep,"
said Gecko.

"The fireflies are flitting all around my house.
They are blinking their lights
        on and off . . .
                on and off . . .
You've got to make them stop.
You're the village boss.
Do something about it."

"I'll talk to the fireflies in the morning,"
said Elephant.
"Now go home and go to bed."

Gecko dragged himself
grumpily home.

"Geck-o . . .
     geck-o . . .
          geck-o . . ."

Next morning Elephant called the fireflies.

"Is it true that you have been flashing your lights
on and off . . . on and off . . . all night long?
Have you been keeping Gecko awake?"

"Oh, yes," said the fireflies.
"We have to blink our lights on and off all night.
 Buffalo leaves his poop all over the road.
 Without our lights, someone would step in the mess!"

"Why, that is very thoughtful of you," said Elephant.
"Just keep on doing what you've been doing.
You can go home now."

So the fireflies went home.

That night at midnight Elephant was awakened again.

"GECK-o! GECK-o! GECK-o!"

Elephant leaned out his window.
"Gecko, go home and go to bed."

"But I can't sleep.
The fireflies are still
blinking their lights
on and off . . .
         on and off . . .
You said you'd make them stop."

"Gecko,
   the fireflies need to blink their lights.
Buffalo leaves poop in the road.
Without their lights
someone might step in it."

"Then talk to Buffalo.
You're the village boss.
Do something about it!"

In the morning Elephant called Buffalo.

"Buffalo, is it true you have been dropping poop all over the road?"

"Oh, yes. Rain washes holes in the road every afternoon.
I just fill them up the best way I know how.
If I didn't do that, someone could
stumble in the holes and get hurt."

"That is very thoughtful of you, Buffalo.
Just keep on doing what you have been doing.
You can go home now."

So Buffalo went home.

That night at midnight Elephant was awakened again.

"GECK-o! GECK-o! GECK-o!"

Elephant leaned out his window.
"Gecko, will you please go home and go to bed?"

"I can't sleep.
The fireflies are still
blinking their lights
on and off . . .
on and off . . .
You said you'd do
something about it!"

"Gecko, let me explain . . .
Buffalo fills up the holes
that Rain washes out.
The fireflies light the road
so no one steps in Buffalo's mess.
You'll just have to
put up with the fireflies."

"Talk to Rain!
You're the village boss.
Do something about it!"

In the morning Elephant called Rain.

"Is it true you wash holes in the road every afternoon?"

"Oh, yes. I rain hard every afternoon
to make puddles for the mosquitoes.
If the puddles dried up,
the mosquitoes would die.
If the mosquitoes died,
there would be nothing for Gecko to eat.
So I rain very hard every day."

"I see," said Elephant.
"Rain, you may go home."

That night at midnight Elephant was awakened.

"GECK-o! GECK-o! GECK-o!"

He leaned out his window.
"Gecko, go home and go to bed!"

"I still can't sleep.
The fireflies are blinking their lights
on and off . . .
on and off . . .
You said you'd do something about it!"

"Gecko, listen carefully. If Rain doesn't rain
every afternoon, there will be no puddles.
If there are no puddles, there will be no
mosquitoes. If there are no mosquitoes,
YOU, Gecko, will have nothing to eat.
Now what do you think of that?"

Gecko thought.

If Elephant told Rain to stop raining,

Buffalo could
stop filling the holes,

and the
fireflies could
stop flashing their lights . . .

but Gecko would have
nothing to eat!'

"Gecko," said Elephant.
"This world is all connected.
Some things you just
have to put up with.
Now go home
and go to
sleep."

So Gecko went home.
Gecko closed his eyes.
Gecko went to sleep.

Outside the fireflies blinked
    on and off . . .
        on and off . . . .

            Some things you just have to put up with.

For Murti, Bun, Suyadi, Made Taro, and my wonderful
storytelling friends at Kelompok Pencinta Bacaan Anak—MRM

To Stela and Dora—GV

TALE NOTE

This story was inspired by a Balinese tale in *Folk Tales from Bali and Lombok* by Margaret Muth Alibasah (Jakarta: Penerbit Djambatan, 1990). The story also is retold by Balinese storyteller Made Taro in his *Lagu-Lagu Permainan Tradisional Bali* (Denpasar: Upada Sastra, 1999). In Made Taro's version, a woodpecker begins the tale and the chief is a lion, rather than a human. Our illustrator, Geraldo Valério, made an artistic decision to depict the village head as an elephant. The tale includes folklore motifs: *J2102 Expensive means of getting rid of insects,* and *Z40 Chains with interdependent members.* In this tale I hope for Gecko's call to echo that of the Indonesian wall gecko's nightly call of TOK-keh!

Text copyright © 2006 by Margaret Read MacDonald.
Illustrations copyright © 2006 by Geraldo Valério.

Published 2006 by August House Publishers, Inc.
P.O. Box 3223, Little Rock, Arkansas, 72203,
501-372-5450, http://www.augusthouse.com

Book design by Joy Freeman
Manufactured in Korea
10 9 8 7 6 5 4 3 2 1

LIBRARY OF CONGRESS CATALOGING-IN-PUBLICATION DATA

MacDonald, Margaret Read, 1940-
    Go to sleep, Gecko! : a Balinese folktale / retold by Margaret Read MacDonald ; illustrated by Geraldo Valério.
        p. cm.
    "This story was inspired by a Balinese tale in Folk tales from Bali and Lombok by Margaret Muth Alibasah (Jakarta: Penerbit Djambatan, 1990)"—Copyright p.
    Summary: Retells the folktale of the gecko who complains to the village chief that the fireflies keep him awake at night but then learns that in nature all things are connected.
    ISBN-13: 978-0-87483-780-3 (hardcover : alk. paper)
    ISBN-10: 0-87483-780-4 (hardcover : alk. paper)
    1. Tales—Indonesia—Bali Island. [1. Folklore—Indonesia—Bali Island.] I. Valerio, Geraldo, ill. II. Title. 010a 2006040748

PZ8.1.M15924Got 2006
398.2—dc22
                                                                                    2006040748

The paper used in this publication meets the minimum requirements of the American National Standard
for Information Sciences—Permanence of Paper for Printed Library Materials, ANSI Z39.48-1984.

AUGUST HOUSE   PUBLISHERS   LITTLE ROCK